NOV 2 5 2008

JE STE
Reader

Maybelle
Goes to Tea

Katie Speck

Illustrations by Paul Rátz de Tagyos

Henry Holt and Company ☺ New York

For Allen, my first reader and best friend

—K. S.

Henry Holt and Company, LLC
Publishers since 1866
175 Fifth Avenue
New York, New York 10010
www.HenryHoltKids.com

Henry Holt® is a registered trademark of Henry Holt and Company, LLC.

Library of Congress Cataloging-in-Publication Data
Speck, Katie.
Maybelle goes to tea / Katie Speck ; illustrations by Paul Rátz de Tagyos.—1st ed.
p.   cm.
Summary: Maybelle the cockroach follows the advice of her new fly
friend Maurice and tumbles into a terrifying but tasty adventure during
Mrs. Peabody's Ladies' Spring Tea.
ISBN-13: 978-0-8050-8093-3 / ISBN-10: 0-8050-8093-7
[1. Cockroaches—Fiction. 2. Insects—Fiction. 3. Afternoon teas—Fiction.]
I. Rátz de Tagyos, Paul, ill. II. Title.
PZ7.S741185Mag 2008   [Fic]—dc22   2007040937

First Edition—2008
Printed in the United States of America on acid-free paper. ∞

1   3   5   7   9   10   8   6   4   2

Contents

Red Hot!

Myrtle and Herbert Peabody were quite sure there were ABSOLUTELY, POSITIVELY NO BUGS in their house at Number 10 Grand Street. That's because Maybelle the Cockroach behaved herself. She obeyed all three of The Rules: *When it's light, stay out of sight; if you're spied, better hide;* and *never meet with human feet.*

1

But there are Cockroach Cautions, too. One night Maybelle ignored a very important one: *Test before you taste.* She found a tiny red spill on the kitchen floor, and she loved food *so* much and got *so* excited that she forgot about the cautions altogether. Nobody's perfect.

"Raspberry jam!" she said to herself. "My favorite thing, after chocolate."

She didn't use her antennae to sniff the spill, and she didn't take a weensy taste. She didn't *test* at all. She dove right in, face first.

She got an unpleasant surprise. It was *not* raspberry jam. It was red-hot pepper sauce. It was *so* hot that she jigged and

danced around the floor. She felt as if she'd eaten a fire ant.

"OH! OUCH!"

Maybelle dashed for the sink and hung upside down off the end of the faucet. She needed a drop of water to cool her mouth parts. But she waited . . . and waited . . . and waited. The faucet didn't leak. Everything was JUST SO at Number 10 Grand Street.

"What are you doing, kiddo?" Henry the Flea said when he hopped by for a visit.

"I'm waiting," Maybelle grumbled. "I'm waiting for this faucet to leak. I'm 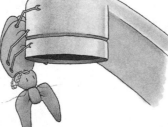 waiting for my mouth to stop burning. I'm waiting for something *delicious.*"

"I'm waiting for a golden retriever," Henry  said. "But I've got a cat. You've got crumbs and spills. We make the best of what we have, remember?"

Maybelle did remember. And she knew that adventures happen to a cockroach who breaks The Rules. She would try to be content eating crumbs and spills in the dark, like any other cockroach. She didn't want an adventure.

But adventure was about to come along anyway. Because whether a cockroach is behaving herself or she isn't, life is full of surprises.

⚙ 2 ⚙

Belly Up

The next morning, Maybelle and Henry watched from Maybelle's home under the refrigerator as the Peabodys hurried out the kitchen door. They were off to buy goodies for Mrs. Peabody's Ladies' Spring Tea. It was an Extra Special occasion. Only the Best People were invited.

But when the Peabodys went out, someone zoomed in without an invitation.

"BRZZZT! Maurice here!" said a very large fly. "Coming in."

As soon as he was in, Maurice began trying to get out. "BRZZZT! Going out."

He wasn't going out. The Peabodys were gone, the door was closed, and a big, noisy fly was trapped in the kitchen.

"Going out! Going out!" Maurice said, throwing himself against the door. "Going out!" he said, crashing into the wall.

"This is going to be trouble," Henry said to Maybelle.

"What will we do?" Maybelle said to Henry.

"BRZZZZZT! Going out!" Maurice cried. And he smacked up against the windowpane so hard that he knocked himself insensible.

Maurice lay on the windowsill with his legs in the air for what seemed a very long time. Even belly-up, he was Noticeable. And Unwelcome. And likely to cause an Extermination Event at Number 10 Grand Street.

"Come on, Maybelle. We've got to hide him before the Peabodys see him and call the Bug Man," Henry said.

"I'm not going out there. What if Ramona the Cat catches me?"

"Don't worry. Ramona is busy bird-watching in an upstairs window."

Maybelle *was* worried, but she didn't want a visit from the Bug Man. So the two friends ventured out into the kitchen.

When it's light, stay out of sight! The day had hardly begun, and Maybelle had already broken The First Cockroach Rule.

☙ 3 ❧

Carry On

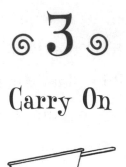

With Henry bouncing along beside her, Maybelle scuttled across the floor and up the wall to the windowsill where Maurice lay.

Maybelle didn't like the look of him. He had bug eyes, hairy legs, and his feet smelled like sour milk. Still, there was nothing to do but get him on her back and carry him home.

Maybelle made herself as flat as she could. "Get under him and push, Henry."

Henry hopped, and panted, and shoved against the big fly. Finally, with a desperate heave, he managed to load Maurice onto Maybelle's back. "To the refrigerator!" he cried.

But before Maybelle had gotten even halfway there, the Peabodys returned. Luckily, they could hardly see over their bulging grocery bags.

"Even Mildred Snodgrass is coming to my Ladies' Spring Tea," Mrs. Peabody said as she struggled into the kitchen. "It will be the social event of the year, Herbert. It must be Extra Special."

"I'm sure it will be perfection, Myrtle," Herbert Peabody said.

Maybelle scrambled frantically among

human feet, darting this way and that. She had to get home as fast as possible. The Peabodys would see her when they put their bags down. If they saw her, the Bug Man would come. If they *stepped* on her . . .

"Hurry!" Henry shouted.

Maybelle hurried so fast that Maurice nearly slid off her back. But she made it to the refrigerator, stuffed him into the crack that was her front door, and followed him in.

"There!" she said. "We'll tell Maurice how things are done around here when he wakes up."

"If you say so, kiddo." Henry sounded doubtful.

⚭ 4 ⚭

Go for It!

Maybelle and Henry watched Mrs. Peabody from Maybelle's door. First she took a teapot with matching cups and saucers from the cupboard. Then she piled platters high with tea cakes, biscuits, and sandwiches with the crusts cut off. And just before she went upstairs to dress for the party, she arranged Chocolate Surprise Cookies on her best plate.

"I wonder what the surprise *is*, Henry.
Don't you?"

"Maybe there'll be crumbs on the
floor tonight and you can find out."

"I want to taste the surprise while it's
still in the cookie," Maybelle said.

"We're making the best of what we have. Remember, kiddo?"

Maybelle remembered. And she wasn't happy about it.

While the two friends talked, Maurice recovered from his crash. He tested his wings. "BZZZRT! Any garbage in here?"

"Certainly not! This is Number 10 Grand Street. Everything here is JUST SO," Maybelle said.

"Yeah, right, right. So what *do* you have to eat, huh?" Maurice rubbed his legs together vigorously. "Any rotten eggs? Moldy cheese? How about some spoiled meat? BZRRRT!" He rubbed his legs faster and faster.

Before Maybelle could answer, he saw the Ladies' Spring Tea spread out on the kitchen counter. Everything was arranged on the plates JUST SO.

"Never mind, Missy. Gonna get me some *goodies!*"

"You can't do that!" Maybelle cried. "There are Rules here. If we don't obey them, the Bug Man comes."

"BRZZZT! I've got my own Rule, Missy," Maurice said. *"Go for it!"*

And he did.

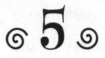

Cockroach Sandwich

"I don't like Maurice," Maybelle said to Henry. "He's very irritating. He's noisy. He rubs his hairy legs together. His feet smell. And he calls me Missy."

"Don't be too hard on him, Maybelle," Henry said. "You never know. Sometimes when you think you couldn't like someone at all, they surprise you."

Maybelle peeked out to see what Maurice was up to. What she didn't like the *most* about him was that he was getting to eat all the delicious treats *she* wanted. He was buzzing and rubbing and treading all over everything with his smelly feet. When he landed on the Chocolate Surprises, Maybelle had had enough.

"This won't do, Henry! Rules or no Rules, I'm going out there!"

Maybelle didn't know that Ramona was no longer bird-watching upstairs— she was crouched in front of the refrigerator. Maybelle barged out of her cozy little home right under the cat's nose.

Ramona's eyes were wide with excitement. *WHAM!* She reached out a paw and whacked Maybelle hard on her bottom. *WHAM!* She whacked her again. It was too late for the terrified cockroach to turn back—the cat blocked her way. So Maybelle bolted forward instead and headed for the counter. Ramona was barely a whisker's length behind her.

"GO! GO!" Henry said.

"BZRRRT!" Maurice stood on the ceiling, watching the chase and rubbing his legs together.

Maybelle jumped on the first plate she came to. She wriggled in between a slice of cucumber and a piece of buttered bread and held her breath.

Ramona swatted at Maybelle's sandwich. "Raaoow!"

"No, Precious!" Mrs. Peabody said, hurrying into the kitchen. "There's nothing in that cucumber sandwich that a kitty would like. It's for the ladies."

Mrs. Peabody put Ramona on the floor, gave her a pat, and took the sandwiches and the other goodies into the parlor.

Maybelle went to her very first Ladies' Spring Tea.

☙ 6 ❧

Teatime

The ladies looked grand. They were powdered and polished and dressed in their best clothes. Mrs. Snodgrass even wore a new hat with decorations piled on top that looked like shiny little fruits—apples and oranges and lemons.

"Why, Myrtle, everything on the tea table is Just So. What lovely treats!" she said.

Maurice agreed. He invited himself to the party and zoomed among the ladies. "BRZZZT!"

Maybelle peeked out of her cucumber sandwich. "Oh, dear," she said to no one in particular.

"Shoo!" Mrs. Peabody cried, flapping her hand at Maurice.

All the ladies joined in, shooing and flapping. Ramona tried to help, too. But Maurice paid them no mind. He was going for it.

Mrs. Peabody's face turned red with embarrassment. She called Mr. Peabody in from the yard. "You must do something, Herbert! Get the fly swatter."

"Let me handle this, ladies," he announced. He began stalking Maurice, fly swatter upraised.

Maurice landed on the biscuits. *BAM!*
Mr. Peabody smashed the biscuits but

missed Maurice. Maurice landed on the
tea cakes. *BAM!* Mr. Peabody crushed
the tea cakes, but Maurice was already
on the cucumber sandwiches.

"Over there!" the ladies urged. Mr.
Peabody was excited by the chase.

Maurice was everywhere at once. *SMACK! SMACK!* When he alighted on Mrs. Snodgrass's hat—*BAM!*—little fruits flew into the air. They hit the floor and bounced and rolled like marbles.

There was a moment of shocked silence. "You've ruined my new hat. I didn't come here to be attacked by filthy insects," Mrs. Snodgrass snapped.

"Anyone could have a fly in the house," Sue Ellen Snerdly said.

Then another of the ladies pointed at a plate. "*That's* a cockroach!"

Maybelle sat stunned and exposed on what was left of the cucumber sandwiches. She wore a piece of buttered bread on her head.

If you're spied, better hide! Maybelle skittered for cover under the carpet. At the sight of a skittering cockroach, the ladies panicked and fled across the little fruits from Mrs. Snodgrass's hat. The fruits rolled, and the ladies slid and slipped and sprawled and crawled to get out of the house.

Mrs. Snerdly regained her feet at the door, straightened her dress, and smiled. "Thank you for the tea party. It was Extra Special. It isn't *so* terrible to have a cockroach in the cucumber sandwiches."

Mrs. Peabody began to sob. Her Ladies' Spring Tea was over.

 7

In a Fog

The only things that managed to survive Mr. Peabody's fly swatter were the Chocolate Surprises and the fly. Maurice buzzed around and enjoyed what was left of the party.

Mrs. Peabody wiped her eyes and blew her nose. "I'm feeling faint, Herbert," she announced.

"Put your head down and breathe, dear. *Breathe!*" Mr. Peabody said.

"My tea party is ruined!" Mrs. Peabody sniffed from between her knees. "Call the Bug Man, Herbert!"

"No need, dear, I'll handle this myself. I'm going to set off a Bug Bomb. We'll wait in the yard. And in a little while there will be absolutely, positively NO BUGS at Number 10 Grand Street."

Mr. Peabody helped Mrs. Peabody outside. He carried Ramona. Mrs. Peabody carried the plate of Chocolate Surprises. "You know I eat when I'm upset, Herbert," she sniffed.

"A little fresh air will do you a world of good, Myrtle."

Mr. Peabody closed all the windows and put a Bug Bomb in the parlor. He pushed the button on the bomb and rushed out into the yard.

One, two, three—the Bug Bomb sent a deadly fog drifting through the house.

Under the carpet, Maybelle's heart raced. "We've got to get out of here, Henry!"

"We can go through Ramona's cat door. But we have to go *now*," Henry said. The white fog was spreading across the parlor, coming closer and closer. "Follow us, Maurice."

Maurice had difficulty taking directions. "BRZZZZT! Going out." He threw himself against the wall. "Going out!" He threw himself against the door. "Going out, going out!" He threw himself against the window with a great *THWACK!* Maurice lay belly-up on the windowsill.

"Not again," Maybelle moaned. "Now what?"

But she knew what had to be done. The poisonous fog drifted their way. There was no time to spare. Little Henry grunted and strained and loaded the fly onto Maybelle's back.

Maybelle didn't care for Maurice, but he was a bug. Bugs stick together—even if one of them is very irritating.

⊙ 8 ⊙

Go for It?

Maybelle and Henry shoved Maurice through the cat door and found themselves in Mr. Peabody's yard.

The outside of Number 10 Grand Street was every bit as JUST SO as the inside. Mr. Peabody kept the grass cut to *exactly* two inches. He clipped all the shrubs into neat balls. And he put a sign on the lawn that said "STAY OFF THE

GRASS: ABSOLUTELY, POSITIVELY NO CHILDREN OR DOGS!" Maybelle thought it might be wise to hide. She and Henry left Maurice on the stoop and crawled under the doormat.

From their hiding place, the two friends watched the Peabodys. The humans sat side by side on lawn chairs with the plate of Chocolate Surprises close at hand.

"Mrs. Snodgrass will never forgive us!" Mrs. Peabody said. "I'm very upset, Herbert." She popped a Surprise into her mouth. "I don't know when I've been so upset." She popped another Surprise into her mouth.

Maybelle looked at the plate of Surprises. Surely, Mrs. Peabody couldn't eat any more. There was only one left now. Maybelle had wondered all morning what the surprise *was*. She might never know. Unless . . .

"I'm going to find out what's in that cookie," Maybelle said.

"You can't do that, kiddo. That would be *really* dangerous. Stay here until it's safe to go back in the house. As for me"—

Henry eyed Ramona, who was settling down for a nap in the sun—"I'm going to get a hot lunch." And he bounded off to his cat.

"Everyone else has something good to eat," Maybelle thought out loud. "I've been in danger all day and I have nothing to show for it. Maybe Maurice has the right idea."

So Maybelle took a deep breath, counted "One, two, three," and rushed out from under the doormat. *"Go for it!"* she cried and made a run at the last cookie.

❧ 9 ❧

Foolish Pleasure

The Peabodys were looking in the other direction. They didn't see Maybelle coming. But Ramona did. She woke up and scratched at the flea behind her ear just as Maybelle charged by.

"Uh-oh. Look out, Maybelle!" Henry shouted. His hot lunch leaped up and began the chase.

With Ramona in pursuit, Maybelle ran until she reached the cookie. And with no time to sniff or taste or test, she plunged into the mysterious heart of the last Chocolate Surprise.

Soft, creamy fudge—that's what she found inside. It wasn't especially surprising. But it was so delicious that she forgot Rules and Cautions and humans and cats.

BOP!

Ramona didn't forget about a certain plump cockroach. *BAT!* She reached out and batted the cookie. Then she batted it some more. *BAT! BAT!*

"Oh my, Herbert. Look at silly Ramona!" Myrtle Peabody said. "She wants my cookie. No, naughty kitty, it's for Mommy. Cookies *comfort* Mommy."

And with that, Mrs. Peabody stuffed the Surprise into her mouth. If she'd bothered to look at it first, she might have noticed that it had legs and a bottom.

☙ 10 ☙

A Chocolate Surprise

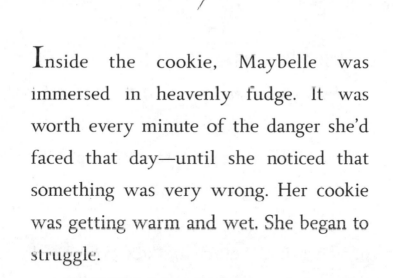

Inside the cookie, Maybelle was immersed in heavenly fudge. It was worth every minute of the danger she'd faced that day—until she noticed that something was very wrong. Her cookie was getting warm and wet. She began to struggle.

"BLECK!" Mrs. Peabody cried at the same moment. "BLECK! BLECK!"

"Whatever is the matter, dear?" Mr.
Peabody said.

"BLECK!" Mrs. Peabody leaped out
of her chair and spit the Chocolate
Surprise out on the grass. "ICK! ICK!
ICK! There's a bug in that cookie! Oh,
bleck! I'm going to faint, Herbert."

Mr. Peabody leaped up and helped
her back into her chair. "Put your head
between your knees, dear, and breathe.
Breathe!"

"But it *moved*, Herbert. I felt its nasty legs!"

"Breathe, dear. I'll handle this." Mr. Peabody stood over the mushy glob of Chocolate Surprise and raised his foot.

Never meet with human feet! It was too late—Maybelle had broken the Third Rule.

Then Mr. Peabody looked at his clean shiny shoe. It wouldn't be JUST SO if he used it to smash a cookie with a bug in it. So he went off to get a more suitable weapon. He came back with a shovel.

"What are you going to do, Herbert?"

"I'm going to scoop up the cookie and throw it over the fence into the neighbor's yard. They won't care about the mess and the bug. They have children and a dog."

So Maybelle sailed over the fence in a wet Surprise and landed at Number 8 Grand Street.

⊙ 11 ⊙

As the Crow Flies

Maybelle squirmed out of the cookie. She was unchewed but very frightened. And she'd had quite enough Surprise for one day. Now she wanted to go home. She was wondering exactly where home was when a shadow fell across her.

Maybelle looked up a long beak into the beady black eyes of a crow. PECK! PECK! Somebody *else* was trying to eat her. She scrambled away, but the bird followed. PECK! HOP! PECK! The faster Maybelle ran, the faster the crow hopped.

Suddenly—HOP, PECK, WHOOSH!—Maybelle was in its beak and soaring into the sky. She squeezed her eyes shut.

When she opened them again, the crow was circling the tree in the backyard of Number 10 Grand Street. In a branch below, Maybelle saw a nest full of baby birds with very big mouths. "*Peep, peep!* Me first!" they all cried at once. The mother crow was about to feed Maybelle to a lucky nestling.

Suddenly, "BRZZT! BRZZT! BRZZZT!" Maurice was everywhere at once. He buzzed around the crow's eyes. He

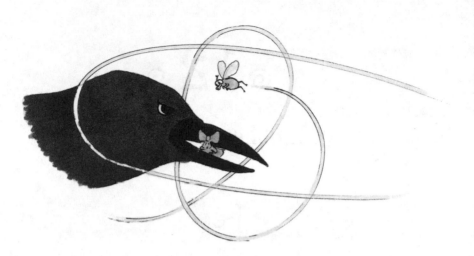

dashed. He dove. He buzzed some more.
He was very, very irritating. The crow
shook its head to shoo him off, but
Maurice paid no attention.

"BRZZZZT! Drop her, girlie!" he
cried. "BRZZZT!" He was *so* irritating that
the crow opened its mouth to protest.

And Maybelle was falling, falling....

☙ 12 ☙

Another Belly, Up

Mrs. Peabody sat slumped in her lawn chair while Mr. Peabody fanned her face. "You've had a horrible experience, Myrtle. But I've taken care of the problem. Try to relax and enjoy the outdoors. There are now absolutely, positively NO BUGS in the yard at Number 10 Grand Street."

Mrs. Peabody had no time to reply. Maybelle landed on her head. *Plop!*

At almost the same moment, "CAW! CAW!" The crow flapped down to snatch Maybelle for her babies. And...

Maurice zoomed around the crow's head to protect Maybelle. "BRZZZT! Scram, birdie!" And...

Ramona saw a cockroach, a bird, and a fly in her mistress's hair, all at once. She crouched. Henry tried to distract the cat by biting her, but she was too excited to notice. "RAUOOOW!" She leaped onto Mrs. Peabody's head.

"EEEEH!" Mrs. Peabody screeched. She jumped up, slapping and swatting at herself. "AWWWK! Falling bugs! Vicious birds! Even Ramona has attacked me! I want to go back inside."

Everyone scattered. The crow flew back to her tree. Maurice zoomed away. Ramona fled across the yard. And Maybelle, for lack of a better idea, hid under Mrs. Peabody's chair.

"I'm going to faint, Herbert," Mrs. Peabody said. But this time she knew just what to do about it. She breathed, and she put her head between her knees. She and Maybelle found themselves looking at each other nose to nose.

Without another word, Mrs. Peabody *did* faint. She somersaulted out of her chair and sprawled belly-up on the grass.

Mr. Peabody was so surprised, he didn't notice Maybelle. "Oh dear!" he said. He fanned his wife's face and patted her cheeks, but she remained insensible. So Mr. Peabody gently loaded Mrs. Peabody into his wheelbarrow and rolled her into the house.

It was safe now. The Bug Bomb had done its work. There were ABSOLUTELY, POSITIVELY NO BUGS at Number 10 Grand Street. Yet.

Maybelle had had quite enough of the outdoors. She wanted to go back inside, too. Henry joined her for the journey home. He kept an eye out for Ramona and the crow while Maybelle talked.

"I'm going to behave from now on," she said. "I'm going to obey The Rules. *Go for it* is not the best idea for a cock-roach. It causes adventures."

At the house, Maybelle scurried across the mat and through the cat door into the kitchen.

The mat said "WELCOME!"

❧ 13 ❧

Red Hot? Not!

The next day, Mrs. Peabody baked a pie.

"I've made my Extra Special Raspberry Rapture as a surprise for Mrs. Snodgrass, Herbert. I know she'll forgive us for ruining her hat when she tastes the pie. It is JUST SO."

"I'm sure it's perfection, dearest. I'll take you out to lunch to celebrate," Mr. Peabody said.

Before they left, Mrs. Peabody opened the kitchen window, closed the screen, and put the pie on the sill to cool. There was no need to cover it. There were no bugs in the house.

Maybelle looked at the pie from her safe little home under the refrigerator. Ripe red raspberries were her favorite thing, after chocolate. And here was a whole pie with a lovely brown crust.

"Where is Ramona?" Maybelle asked Henry.

"She's outside under the tree staring at the crow's nest."

"Well, in that case," said Maybelle, "I'm going to have a taste of the Raspberry Rapture Pie."

Henry didn't point out that Maybelle had promised to obey The Rules only the day before. After all, he thought, nobody's perfect.

Maybelle walked around on the pie. She sniffed and tasted and tested. Then she settled down in the center and began to eat. The pie *was* perfection.

"I like Maurice," she said between bites. "He was nice, wasn't he? I mean, except for his eyes and his feet and his hairy legs and some other things. It's awfully quiet around here without him."

"Just like I said, kiddo. Sometimes, when you think you couldn't like someone at all, they surprise you."

"BZZZRT!" *WHAM!* Maurice hit the window screen. "Hey, Missy!" He rubbed his legs together. "Got anything rotten in there?"

Maybelle was happy to see him. "Certainly not," she said, "but you could come in the cat door and share this pie with me."

"No, thanks. Better stuff across the fence—moldy peanut butter sandwiches, rotten banana peels, dog p—"

"Ssssh! There's a lady present," said Henry.

"Oh, right, right! Gotta go. Kid at Number 8 just dropped an ice cream cone. Gotta get to it before the ants do. BRZZZZT!" Maurice was gone.

"I think I'll go next door for a bite, too," Henry said. "That dog over there could be a golden retriever. You never know."

Maybelle ate Mrs. Snodgrass's Extra Special Raspberry Rapture Pie and thought about life. Henry was right. You never know. She certainly never expected to have a noisy, irritating friend with bug eyes, hairy legs, and smelly feet. But she did. And she might even learn to like being called Missy. Missy Maybelle.

She rubbed her front legs together and had another bite of pie.

One thing is for sure, she decided. Whether you're behaving yourself or you're not, life is full of surprises.